DISCARD

Winter Hunting

FOX

Living in a Shoe

BIG FAMILY BOOKS

LOST SHEEP

BO-PEEP

How to build a BRIDGE

London Bridge Books

NO LONGER PROPERTY OF THE LONG BEACH PUBLIC LIBRARY

Jack Nimble

WORKOUT TAPE

"'It followed her to school one day, which was against the rules.'

Does anybody know what happens next?

Anybody?
No?

READ ACROSS
America

READING
Is
FUN

Well, she found a giant egg crushing the school. It wasn't just any egg, oh no. It was an . . .

EGG-CEEDINGLY Large
HUMPTY DUMPTY."

For Emily,
my editor

All rights reserved. No part of this book may be reproduced or transmitted in any form or by any means, electronic or mechanical, including photocopying, recording, or by any information storage and retrieval system, without permission in writing from the Publisher.

First published in the United States of America in 2001 by Walker Publishing Company, Inc.
Published simultaneously in Canada by Fitzhenry and Whiteside, Markham, Ontario L3R 4T8

Library of Congress Cataloging-in-Publication Data

O'Malley, Kevin, 1961–
   Humpty Dumpty egg-splodes / Kevin O'Malley.
      p.   cm.
   Summary: An enormous Humpty Dumpty returns to seek revenge on the
   nursery rhyme characters who let him fall.
   ISBN 0-8027-8756-8 (hc) — ISBN 0-8027-8757-6 (rein)
   [1. Nursery rhymes—Fiction. 2. Characters in literature—Fiction.] I. Title:
   PZ7.O526 Hu 2001
   [FIC]—dc21

                                           00-043777

Book design by Sophie Ye Chin

Printed in Hong Kong
10 9 8 7 6 5 4 3 2 1

"Humpty Dumpty," said Mary, "what happened to you? You're huge!"

"That's right, I'm huge, and I'm not gonna take it anymore."

"What are you talking about?" asked Mary.

"Oh, you know darn well. 'Oh look, the tubby bald eggman is falling off the wall, haa, haa, haa.' Did anybody ever think how painful it would be to have a horse try to put you back together?

No.

So I'm back, baby."

Say good-bye to Mother Goose Land!

Old King Cole was a merry old soul until Jack came running in.
"What? Humpty Dumpty's gonna wreck the town?" exclaimed the king.
"What am I supposed to do? I'm not a smart king, just a merry one.
The real brains of the town is Mother Goose,
and she's away on vacation getting her feathers fluffed."

"Well, you'd better think of something quick," said Jack.
"Humpty Dumpty's headed this way!"

"I've got it," said Old King Cole. "Get me Peter Piper."

"Peter Piper," said the king. "Pick me a peck of pickled peppers.
Then throw them at Humpty Dumpty.
He hates pickled peppers."

"Your Highness, it didn't work. Humpty just ate the peppers," reported Jack.

"How many pecks of pickled peppers
did Peter Piper pick?" asked the king.

"He pitched pickled peppers until he was positively pooped.
Should I try calling Mother Hubbard?" asked Jack.

"Naw, what's she got to throw at Humpty?
Her cupboard is always bare.
Besides, she's never at home and you'd end up talking to that smart aleck dog.
Let's call the grand old Duke of York," said the king.

Good idea!
He's got ten
thousand men.

"No good, Sire," said Jack. "He marched them all straight up the hill and he marched them down again."

"I should have known," said the king.

"I could try the Old Woman That Lives in the Shoe," said Jack.

"Naw, she's got so many children,
 she won't know what to do," said the king.

"**Sire?**" yelled Jack, "Come quick! Humpty's crashing through the town!"

Humpty Dumpty was on a rampage.
He found Jack Horner sitting in the corner.
He stole his plum, Christmas pie and all.

He sat on Little Miss Muffet's tuffet
and ate all her curds and whey.
He shook the whole town.
Things were looking bad.

"I've got it," said Old King Cole.
"You know Peter . . . Peter Pumpkin Eater?"

"Oh sure. I heard his wife got out of the pumpkin shell. I believe she's doing very well," said Jack.

"Yes, yes, yes. Go and tell Peter to roll that pumpkin downtown.
I want him to stuff Humpty in it."

"I've got it!" barked Old King Cole. "Do you know the Muffin Man?"

"The Muffin Man?" asked Jack.

"The Muffin Man! Do you know the Muffin Man?" asked the king.

"Oh sure," said Jack, "he lives on Drurey Lane."

"Well, go to him and tell him to lay a path of muffins down Main Street.
Tell him to make a left onto Wall Street.
We'll drive Humpty Dumpty right up the wall," said the king.

> Roses are red,
> violets are blue.
> Pumpkins
> are orange,
> and the town is too.

Wrecking a town is hard work. Humpty was really hungry.
He followed the muffin trail just as Old King Cole had hoped.
The enraged eggman climbed right up the wall and sat there eating a huge pile of muffins.

"Now we have to find a way to push him off. That'll knock some sense into him," said the king.

"Sire, Sire! Dr. Foster, on his way to Gloucester, reports that Mother Goose is on her way back home," said Jack.

"Thank goodness," said Old King Cole. "Now I can get back to being merry."

Mother Goose flew in the window.
"The town's a mess. What's going on here?
I can't even go away for the weekend without this place going to pieces."
Old King Cole filled Mother Goose in about Humpty Dumpty's rampage.

"Get me all the king's horses and all the king's men," yelled Mother Goose.
"Send them all to the wall!"

"Yes Ma'am!" said Jack.

Meanwhile,

Humpty was almost finished with his muffins.
He was extremely full.
He was getting very sleepy.
His eyes were beginning to close.
He started to slip off the wall.

Humpty Dumpty sat on the wall.
Humpty Dumpty had a great fall.
All the king's horses
and all the king's men . . .

held out a giant sheet and caught him.

"What are you going to do with him now?" asked Jack.

"Get me Gregory Griggs."

"Gregory Griggs?
Had twenty-seven different wigs?
He wore them up, he wore them down
to please the people of the town?" asked Jack.

"Yes, yes, yes. Now tell him to bring all his wigs," said Mother Goose.

Mother Goose stitched all the wigs together
and gently lowered the hair onto Humpty's head.

With his egg-citing new look and attitude, Humpty Dumpty became a big star.
He does two shows a day and when he falls, the crowd goes wild.

SLEEP DISORDERS

Dr. Little Boy Blue

Good Garden

MARY
CONTRARY PUB

My Life with Dog

Old Woman

SAGA PUB

TOM, TOM...
THE
PIPER'S
SON

Make Pies CHEAP!

VOL. 1

SIMPLE SIMON
VIDEO

This book belongs to

....

First Dictionary

make
believe
ideas

How to use this dictionary

You can use a dictionary to find the meaning of a word or to check how to spell it. Use this page to find out how to get the most from your dictionary.

Letter heading

Heading letters like this one show you where each new letter begins.

Uppercase alphabet panel

Use these panel letters when you are scanning the book to find the right page. The bold letter tells you which letter the words on the page begin with.

Headword

Each entry starts with a headword. These words are in alphabetical order (this is explained at the back of the book). You can use the headwords to check how a word is spelled.

Part of speech

This tells you if a word is a *noun*, *adjective*, or *verb*. (See the final page to learn what these words mean.)

A B C D E F G H I J K L M N O P Q R S T U V W X Y Z

ladder (noun)

A **ladder** is something you use to climb up high. Ladders are made of metal or wood.

lamb (noun)

A **lamb** is a young sheep that is still with its mother.

lamb (noun)

A **lamb** is a yo still with its mo

lamp (noun)

A **lamp** is a device that gives you light. You can move a lamp around and switch it on and off.

large (adjective)
larger, largest
Opposites of **large** are **small** and **tiny**.

If something is **large**, it is big. A hippo is large.

late (adjective)
later, latest
The opposite of **late** is **early**.

To be **late** is to get somewhere after the right time.

BUS STOP

SCHOOL BUS   STOP

Definition

The definition tells you what the word means.

Plurals

Some words have unusual plurals. You can find out how to spell them here. (Learn more about plurals at the back of the book.)

Lowercase alphabet panel

This panel shows the lowercase letters. Use it to find entries in the same way as you use the uppercase panel.

Tenses

Verbs change depending on whether we are talking about the past, the present, or the future. These words tell you the forms to use. For example:

She *will laugh* at the joke.

She *laughs* at the joke.

She *is laughing* at the joke.

She *laughed* at the joke.

laugh (verb)
laughs, laughing, laughed
To **laugh** is to make noises because you think something is funny.

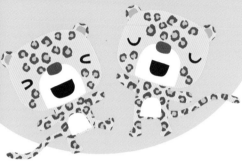

leaf (noun)
leaves
A **leaf** is a flat, green part of a plant, such as a tree.

lazy (adjective)
lazier, laziest
The opposites of **lazy** are **hardworking** and **active**.
To be **lazy** is to not want to do work or exercise.

leg (noun)
Your **legs** are the long parts of your body between your bottom and your feet.

Words for comparing

We use special words to compare things. You can find out how to spell them here. For example:

This boy is *lazy*.

This boy is *lazier* than that one.

This boy is the *laziest* of them all.

DICTIONARY DETECTIVE

What letter change turns a **lamp** into a **lamb**?

lemon (noun)
A **lemon** is a juicy, yellow fruit with a sour taste.

a b c d e f g h i j k l m n o p q r s t u v w x y z

Activities

Some pages have fun activities like this. Doing them helps you learn more about words and how to use a dictionary.

Illustrations

Use the illustrations to help you learn the meaning of a word.

address (noun)
addresses

An **address** is the house number, road, and place where someone lives.

MAIN STREET

airplane (noun)

An **airplane** is a flying machine with wings that carries people and things.

alien (noun)

An **alien** is a make-believe creature from another planet.

alligator (noun)

An **alligator** is a large, scaly animal that lives in rivers and other wet places.

alphabet (noun)

An **alphabet** is a collection of letters that is arranged in a special order.

ambulance (noun)

An **ambulance** is a van that takes people to hospital when they are hurt or sick.

angry (adjective)
angrier, angriest

If you feel **angry**, you feel very upset and annoyed.

animal (noun)

An **animal** is a living thing that moves around. A plant is not an animal. Cats, chickens, spiders, and goldfish are all animals.

ankle (noun)

Your **ankle** is the part of your body where your foot joins your leg.

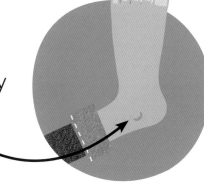

ant (noun)

An **ant** is a small insect that lives and works in a large group.

DICTIONARY DETECTIVE

Can you put these words in alphabetical order?

angry   ant   alien

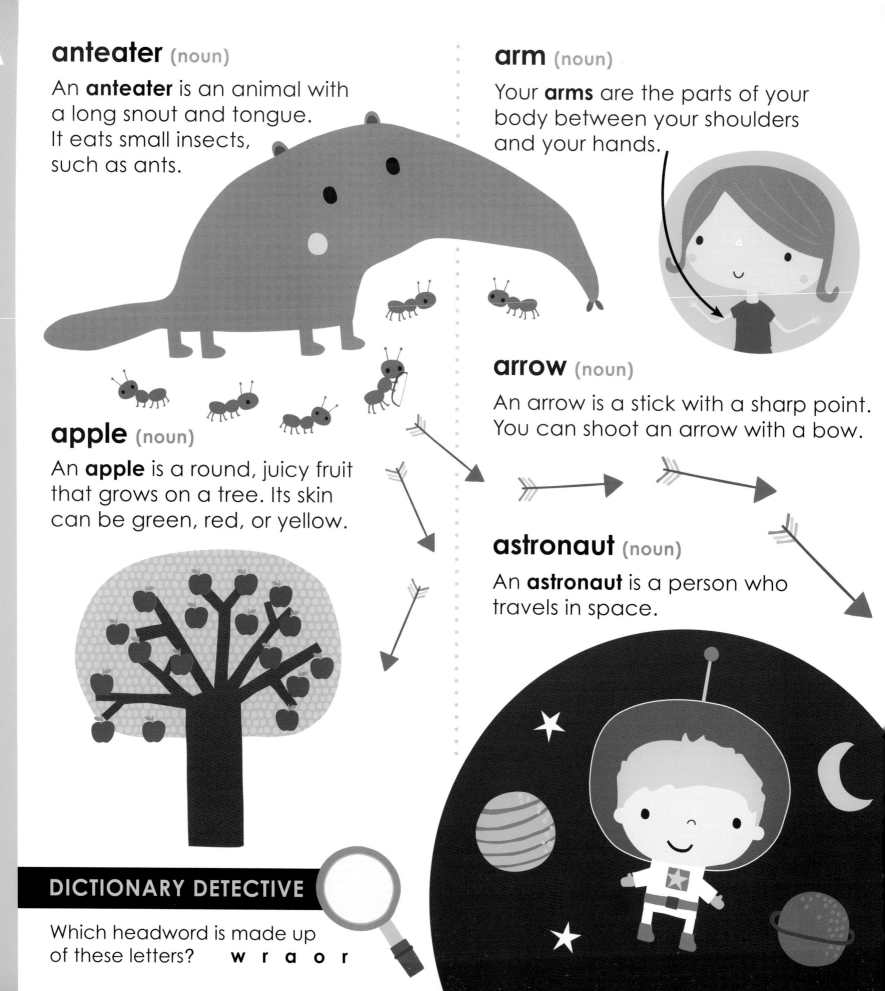

A
B
C
D
E
F
G
H
I
J
K
L
M
N
O
P
Q
R
S
T
U
V
W
X
Y
Z

anteater (noun)

An **anteater** is an animal with a long snout and tongue. It eats small insects, such as ants.

apple (noun)

An **apple** is a round, juicy fruit that grows on a tree. Its skin can be green, red, or yellow.

arm (noun)

Your **arms** are the parts of your body between your shoulders and your hands.

arrow (noun)

An **arrow** is a stick with a sharp point. You can shoot an arrow with a bow.

astronaut (noun)

An **astronaut** is a person who travels in space.

DICTIONARY DETECTIVE

Which headword is made up of these letters? **w r a o r**

Bb

baby (noun)
babies

A **baby** is a very young person.

ball (noun)

A **ball** is a round object used in games. You can throw, catch, bounce, roll, or kick a ball.

banana (noun)

A **banana** is a long fruit with a thick, yellow skin.

basket (noun)

A **basket** is a container used to store or carry things. Baskets are often made by weaving.

bat (noun)

1. A **bat** is a piece of wood that is used to hit a ball in a game.

2. A **bat** is a furry animal with wings that flies at night.

a
b
c
d
e
f
g
h
i
j
k
l
m
n
o
p
q
r
s
t
u
v
w
x
y
z

A B C D E F G H I J K L M N O P Q R S T U V W X Y Z

beach (noun)
beaches

A **beach** is a sandy or pebbly strip of land at the edge of the ocean.

bear (noun)

A **bear** is a large, strong, furry animal that lives in the wild.

beautiful (adjective)
more beautiful, most beautiful

If something is **beautiful**, it looks or sounds lovely.

bed (noun)

A **bed** is something you rest and sleep in.

bee (noun)

A **bee** is an insect with wings. Bees make honey.

beetle (noun)

A **beetle** is an insect with hard, shiny wing covers.

best (adjective)
good, better, best

If something is the **best**, it is better than all others.

bicycle (noun)

A **bicycle** is a vehicle you ride. It has two wheels and pedals.

DICTIONARY DETECTIVE

Which headword rhymes with these words?

wig   fig   twig

big (adjective)
bigger, biggest
The opposite of **big** is **small**.

If something is **big**, it is large. An elephant is big.

bird (noun)

A **bird** is an animal with wings, feathers, and a beak. Most birds can fly.

a
b
c
d
e
f
g
h
i
j
k
l
m
n
o
p
q
r
s
t
u
v
w
x
y
z

A B C D E F G H I J K L M N O P Q R S T U V W X Y Z

birthday (noun)

Your **birthday** is the day of the year you were born.

black (adjective)
blacker, blackest

Black is a color. This cat is black.

blue (adjective)
bluer, bluest

Blue is a color. This truck is blue.

boat (noun)

A **boat** floats on water and carries people and things.

body (noun)
bodies

The **body** of a person or an animal is every part of them.

book (noun)

A **book** is made up of many pages held together inside a cover.

boot (noun)

A **boot** is a shoe that fits over your foot and part of your leg.

box (noun)
boxes

A **box** is used to hold things. Most boxes have straight sides and are made of plastic or cardboard.

boy (noun)

A **boy** is a child who will grow up to be a man.

bread (noun)

Bread is a food made with flour. It is baked in an oven.

DICTIONARY DETECTIVE

What letter change turns a **book** into a **boot**?

a **b** c d e f g h i j k l m n o p q r s t u v w x y z

breakfast (noun)

Breakfast is a meal eaten in the morning. Many people have cereal for breakfast.

bridge (noun)

A **bridge** is a structure built over a river or road. We use it to cross to the other side.

broccoli (noun)

Broccoli is a green vegetable.

brush (noun)
brushes

A **brush** has lots of stiff hairs or wires and usually has a handle.

bucket (noun)

A **bucket** is used to carry things, such as liquids or sand.

bulldozer (noun)

A **bulldozer** is a big machine with a curved blade that pushes rocks out of the way.

butterfly (noun)
butterflies

A **butterfly** is an insect with large, colorful wings.

bus (noun)
buses

A **bus** is a long vehicle with seats inside to carry people around.

SCHOOL BUS

STOP

button (noun)

A **button** is a small object that fastens clothes together.

DICTIONARY DETECTIVE

Which headword has the word **fly** in it?

buy (verb)
buys, buying, bought

To **buy** something is to pay money for it so you can own it.

a b c d e f g h i j k l m n o p q r s t u v w x y z

cake (noun)

A **cake** is a sweet food. It is often made by mixing butter, sugar, eggs, and flour, and then baking the mix in an oven.

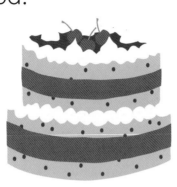

calf (noun)
calves

A **calf** is a baby cow or bull. Baby elephants and baby whales are also called calves.

call (verb)
calls, calling, called

1. To **call** someone is to shout out to them so that they come.

2. To **call** someone means to phone them.

car (noun)

A **car** is a vehicle with four wheels and an engine. We use cars to get from one place to another.

carrot (noun)

A **carrot** is a long, orange vegetable that grows under the ground.

cat (noun)

A **cat** is a four-legged animal with soft fur, sharp claws, and a long tail. People keep small cats as pets.

catch (verb)

catches, catching, caught

To **catch** something is to grab hold of it while it is moving.

caterpillar (noun)

A **caterpillar** is a long, thin insect. It grows into a butterfly or a moth.

cereal (noun)

1. A **cereal** is the grain, or seeds, from a plant such as wheat, corn, or rice.

2. A **cereal** is a breakfast food made from wheat, rice, or oats. You often eat with milk.

chair (noun)

A **chair** is a seat with four legs and a back.

DICTIONARY DETECTIVE

Which word is correct?

He **catched / caught** the ball with one hand.

a b **C** d e f g h i j k l m n o p q r s t u v w x y z

cheese (noun)

Cheese is a food made from milk.

child (noun)
children

A **child** is a boy or girl who has not yet grown up.

chocolate (noun)

Chocolate is a sweet food made from cocoa beans.

milk CHOCO

circle (noun)

A **circle** is a perfectly round shape. Wheels are circle shaped.

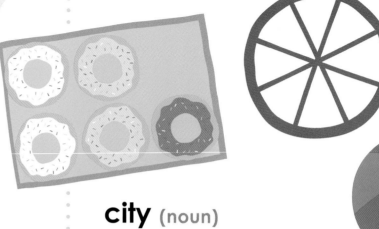

city (noun)
cities

A **city** is a big, busy place where many people live.

clean (verb)
cleans, cleaning, cleaned

To **clean** something is to wash it so that it is no longer dirty.

clock (noun)

A **clock** is a machine that shows you what time it is.

DICTIONARY DETECTIVE

These headwords are spelled wrong. Can you correct them?

clok   cleen   citi

clothes (noun)

Clothes are the things that people wear, such as shirts, trousers, and socks.

coat (noun)

A **coat** is something you wear over other clothes. It keeps you warm when you are outside.

cold (adjective)
colder, coldest
The opposite of **cold** is **hot**.

If something is not warm or hot, it is **cold**. Ice cream is cold.

a b **C** d e f g h i j k l m n o p q r s t u v w x y z

color (noun)

Red, blue, and yellow are **colors**. By mixing them together, you get other colors.

comb (noun)

A **comb** is a piece of plastic or metal that has lots of thin teeth. You use a comb to untangle your hair.

computer (noun)

A **computer** is a machine that stores information and helps people work and keep in contact.

cow (noun)

A **cow** is a large female farm animal that produces milk. The male animal is called a bull, and the baby is a calf.

crawl (verb)
crawls, crawling, crawled

To **crawl** is to move around on your hands and knees. Babies crawl before they can walk.

crocodile (noun)

A **crocodile** is a scaly animal that looks like an alligator. It has sharp teeth, short legs, and a long tail.

crown (noun)

A **crown** is a kind of hat, usually worn by kings and queens. It is often made of gold or silver.

cry (verb)
cries, crying, cried

To **cry** is to be so sad or hurt that tears fall from your eyes.

cup (noun)

A **cup** is a small, round container with a handle. You drink from a cup.

cut (verb)
cuts, cutting, cut

To **cut** something is to open or break into it using scissors or a knife.

DICTIONARY DETECTIVE

Which headword rhymes with these words?

now   how   wow

a b **C** d e f g h i j k l m n o p q r s t u v w x y z

A
B
C
D
E
F
G
H
I
J
K
L
M
N
O
P
Q
R
S
T
U
V
W
X
Y
Z

Dd

dark (adjective)
darker, darkest
The opposite of **dark** is **light**.

If something is **dark**, it is not light or pale. Black is a dark color. It is dark outside at night.

deep (adjective)
deeper, deepest
The opposite of **deep** is **shallow**.

If something is **deep**, its bottom is a long way down. A pool or a hole can be deep.

dentist (noun)
A **dentist** looks after people's teeth.

desert (noun)
A **desert** is a dry place without many plants.

dessert (noun)
A **dessert** is a sweet food you eat at the end of a meal.

diamond (noun)

A **diamond** is a shape with four sides. Some kites are diamond shaped.

die (noun)
dice

A **die** is a small cube with a different number of spots on each side. Dice are used in many games.

dinner (noun)

Dinner is the biggest meal of the day. It is often eaten in the evening.

dinosaur (noun)

A **dinosaur** is a kind of animal that lived millions of years ago.

dirty (adjective)
dirtier, dirtiest
The opposite of **dirty** is **clean**.

If something is **dirty**, it has mud or stains on it.

DICTIONARY DETECTIVE

Which word is correct?

We saw camels in the **dessert / desert**?

a b c **d** e f g h i j k l m n o p q r s t u v w x y z

dish (noun)
dishes

A **dish** is a bowl for serving food.

doctor (noun)

A **doctor** is someone who takes care of people who are sick or hurt, helping them to get better.

dog (noun)

A **dog** is a four-legged animal that is often kept as a pet. Most dogs bark.

donkey (noun)

A **donkey** is a furry animal that looks like a small horse with big ears.

draw (verb)
draws, drawing, drew, drawn

To **draw** is to use pencils, pens, or crayons to make a picture.

dream (noun)

A **dream** is a story you think up while you are asleep.

dress (noun)
dresses

A **dress** is something you wear that has a top part joined to a skirt.

drill (noun)

A **drill** is a tool with a long, thin point that spins around to make holes in things.

drink (verb)
drinks, drinking, drank, drunk

To **drink** is to swallow a liquid, such as water, milk, or juice.

dry (adjective)
drier, driest
The opposite of **dry** is **wet**.

If something is **dry**, it has no water in or on it. You use a hair dryer to make your hair dry.

DICTIONARY DETECTIVE

Can you put these words in alphabetical order?

drink   draw   drill

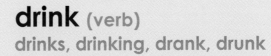

a b c **d** e f g h i j k l m n o p q r s t u v w x y z

Ee

eagle (noun)

An **eagle** is a large bird with big wings, a curved beak, and sharp claws.

ear (noun)

Your **ears** are on each side of your head. You hear with your ears.

early (adjective)
earlier, earliest
The opposite of **early** is **late**.

To be **early** is to get somewhere before you need to be there.

Earth (noun)

1. The planet we live on is called **Earth**. It is also called the world.

2. Another word for soil is **earth**.

easy (adjective)
easier, easiest
The opposite of **easy** is **hard**.

If something is **easy**, you can do it quickly, without trying very hard.

DICTIONARY DETECTIVE

Which headword is made up of these letters? **b w l e o**

eat (verb)
eats, eating, ate, eaten

To **eat** is to chew and swallow food.

egg (noun)

Many animals, such as birds, lizards, and some fish, live inside **eggs** until they are big enough to hatch out.

elbow (noun)

Your **elbow** is the part of your body in the middle of your arm. It allows you to bend your arm.

elephant (noun)

An **elephant** is a large, gray animal with tusks, big ears, and a long nose, called a trunk.

embarrassed (adjective)
more embarrassed, most embarrassed

If you feel **embarrassed**, you feel bad or foolish about something you said or did.

a b c d **e** f g h i j k l m n o p q r s t u v w x y z

A B C D **E** F G H I J K L M N O P Q R S T U V W X Y Z

empty (adjective)
emptier, emptiest
The opposite of **empty** is **full**.

If something is **empty**, it has nothing inside it.

envelope (noun)

An **envelope** is a paper cover, or container, you put letters or cards inside.

evening (noun)

The **evening** is the time between the afternoon and nighttime. In the evening, it starts to get dark.

DICTIONARY DETECTIVE

Which word is correct?

Two **familys / families** visited the farm.

exercise (verb)
exercises, exercising, exercised

To **exercise** is to move your body to keep it fit and healthy.

eye (noun)

Your **eyes** are on your face. You see with your eyes.

face (noun)

Your **face** is the front part of your head. Your eyes, nose, and mouth are all part of your face.

fall (verb)
falls, falling, fell, fallen

To **fall** is to trip or drop down onto the ground by mistake.

farm (noun)

A **farm** is a place where farmers grow food and raise animals.

family (noun)
families

Your **family** is the group of people closest to you. Your parents, sisters, and brothers are all part of your family even if you don't live together.

fast (adjective)
faster, fastest
The opposite of **fast** is **slow**.

To be **fast** is to be doing something quickly. Race cars are fast cars.

a b c d e **f** g h i j k l m n o p q r s t u v w x y z

A
B
C
D
E
F
G
H
I
J
K
L
M
N
O
P
Q
R
S
T
U
V
W
X
Y
Z

fat (adjective)
fatter, fattest
The opposite of **fat** is **thin**.

To be **fat** is to have a large, wide body.

father (noun)

A **father** is a man who has children.

feather (noun)

Birds have **feathers** on their bodies to keep them warm and dry. Feathers are light and help birds fly.

finger (noun)

Your **fingers** are the long, thin parts of your hand. Each hand has four fingers and a thumb.

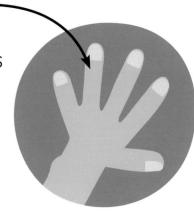

fire (noun)

A **fire** is the hot, bright flames and smoke made when something is burning.

DICTIONARY DETECTIVE

Can you put these words in alphabetical order?

fix   fire   fish

fire truck (noun)

Fire trucks are the vehicles firefighters use to drive to fires.

fish (noun)
fish, fishes

A **fish** is a type of animal that lives in water. Fish have fins to swim and gills to "breathe" underwater.

fix (verb)
fixes, fixing, fixed

To **fix** something broken is to put it back together or mend it so that it works again.

flower (noun)

A **flower** is the part of a plant with petals. Many flowers smell nice and have bright colors.

fly (verb)
flies, flying, flew, flown

To **fly** is to move through the air without touching the ground. Birds, planes, and helicopters fly.

A
B
C
D
E
F
G
H
I
J
K
L
M
N
O
P
Q
R
S
T
U
V
W
X
Y
Z

food (noun)

Food is what you eat. It keeps you strong and healthy.

foot (noun)
feet

Your **foot** is the part of your body that touches the ground. It has five toes.

forest (noun)

A **forest** is a large area with many trees growing together.

fork (noun)

A **fork** is a tool used for eating. It has sharp, pointed ends and a handle.

fowl (noun)

Fowl are birds such as chickens, ducks, and turkeys that people farm for their eggs and meat.

fox (noun)
foxes

A **fox** is a reddish brown forest animal with a bushy tail.

DICTIONARY DETECTIVE

What letter change turns **food** into a **foot**?

Friday (noun)

Friday is the fifth day of the school week. It is the day before the weekend.

MONDAY	TUESDAY	WEDNESDAY	THURSDAY	FRIDAY	SATURDAY	SUNDAY
	1	2	3	4	5	6
7	8	9	10	11	12	13
14	15	16	17	18	19	20
21	22	23	24	25	26	27
28	29	30	31			

friend (noun)

A **friend** is a person you like and want to spend time with. A friend likes you, too.

frog (noun)

A **frog** is a small animal that lives in damp places. It has large back legs and can jump far.

fruit (noun)

A **fruit** is a part of a plant that holds seeds. Many fruits, such as apples and grapes, are juicy and good to eat.

full (adjective)
fuller, fullest
The opposite of **full** is **empty**.

If something is **full**, it has so much in it that there is no more room.

a b c d e f g h i j k l m n o p q r s t u v w x y z

Gg

game (noun)

A **game** is something you play for fun. Chutes and Ladders is a game.

garden (noun)

A **garden** is a place where people grow grass and other plants.

gate (noun)

A **gate** is a type of door in a wall, fence, or hedge.

gentle (adjective)
gentler, gentlest
The opposite of **gentle** is **rough**.

To be **gentle** is to treat someone or something with care and kindness.

giraffe (noun)

A **giraffe** is a tall animal with a spotted coat and a very long neck.

girl (noun)

A **girl** is a child who will grow up to be a woman.

glasses (noun)

People wear **glasses** over their eyes to see better or to protect their eyes from the sun.

goat (noun)

A **goat** is an animal with long hair and horns on its head. It looks a bit like a sheep.

grandfather (noun)

A **grandfather** is a man whose children are grown and have children of their own.

grandmother (noun)

A **grandmother** is a woman whose children are grown and have children of their own.

DICTIONARY DETECTIVE

Which two headwords contain the word **grand**?

a b c d e f g h i j k l m n o p q r s t u v w x y z

ABCDEFG HIJKLMNOPQRSTUVWXYZ

grape (noun)

A **grape** is a small purple or green fruit that grows in bunches. Grapes are used to make wine.

green (adjective)
greener, greenest

Green is a color. Grass and leaves are green.

grow (verb)
grows, growing, grew, grown

When somebody or something **grows**, it gets bigger.

grumpy (adjective)
grumpier, grumpiest
The opposite of **grumpy** is **cheerful**.

To feel **grumpy** is to be cross and to feel like complaining.

gymnastics (noun)

Gymnastics is a sport and exercise in which you use strength and balance to do different movements.

Hh

hair (noun)

Your **hair** is made up of all the long, thin strands that grow on top of your head.

half (noun)
halves

When something is broken into two pieces the same size, one piece is called a **half**.

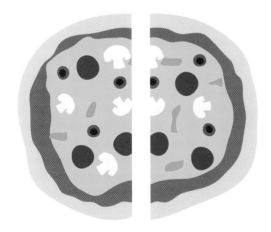

DICTIONARY DETECTIVE

Can you put these words in alphabetical order?

hamster   hammer   hair

hammer (noun)

A **hammer** is a tool you can use to pound nails into wood.

hamster (noun)

A **hamster** is a small, furry animal with a short tail. Some people keep hamsters as pets.

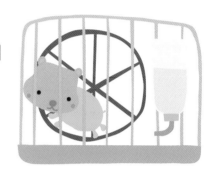

hand (noun)

Your **hand** is the part of your body that is at the end of your arm. It has five fingers.

a b c d e f g **h** i j k l m n o p q r s t u v w x y z

A B C D E F G H I J K L M N O P Q R S T U V W X Y Z

happy (adjective)
happier, happiest
The opposite of **happy** is **sad**.

To feel **happy** is to feel joyful or pleased.

hard (adjective)
harder, hardest
The opposites of **hard** are **soft** and **easy**.

1. If something is **hard**, it is firm and does not squash easily.
2. If something is **hard**, it is tricky or difficult to do.

DICTIONARY DETECTIVE

Which headword rhymes with these words?

near fear tear

hat (noun)
A **hat** is something you wear on your head.

head (noun)

Your **head** is the part of your body that is above your neck.

hear (verb)
hears, hearing, heard

To **hear** something is to pick up its sounds with your ears.

heart (noun)

1. Your **heart** is in your chest. It pumps blood around your body.

2. A **heart** is a shape that stands for love.

heavy (adjective)
heavier, heaviest
The opposite of **heavy** is **light**.

If something is **heavy**, it weighs a great deal and is hard to carry.

helicopter (noun)

A **helicopter** is a flying machine with blades that spin around. It can move straight up from the ground and hover in one place.

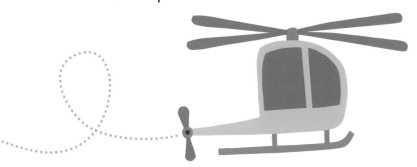

help (verb)
helps, helping, helped

To **help** someone is to do something to make things easier or better for them.

hide (verb)
hides, hiding, hid, hidden

To **hide** something is to put it where other people cannot find it. You can hide a thing or you can hide yourself.

a b c d e f g h i j k l m n o p q r s t u v w x y z

A B C D E F **G H** I J K L M N O P Q R S T U V W X Y Z

hollow (adjective)
hollower, hollowest

If something is **hollow**, it is empty inside. A balloon is hollow.

hop (verb)
hops, hopping, hopped

You **hop** when you jump up and down on one leg.

horse (noun)

A **horse** is a big animal with hooves. People ride horses and use them to pull heavy loads.

hot (adjective)
hotter, hottest
The opposite of **hot** is **cold**.

If something is not cold or warm, it is **hot**. Hot things can burn you.

house (noun)

A **house** is a building where people eat, sleep, and live. Houses have roofs, walls, doors, and windows to keep the people inside warm and dry.

hug (verb)
hugs, hugging, hugged

To **hug** someone is to put your arms around them.

DICTIONARY DETECTIVE

Which word is correct?

Hannah **huged / hugged** her horse.

ice (noun)

Ice is frozen water.
It is cold, hard, and slippery.

ice cream (noun)

Ice cream is a sweet, creamy frozen food made from milk.

igloo (noun)

An **igloo** is a small, round house made from blocks of ice.

insect (noun)

An **insect** is a small animal with three body parts and six legs. Many insects have wings. Ants, beetles, butterflies, and bees are all insects.

iron (noun)

An **iron** is a heavy tool with a hot base. It is used to remove wrinkles from clothes.

a b c d e f g h **i** j k l m n o p q r s t u v w x y z

A B C D E F G H I J K L M N O P Q R S T U V W X Y Z

Jj

jacket (noun)

A **jacket** is a short coat that people wear to keep warm.

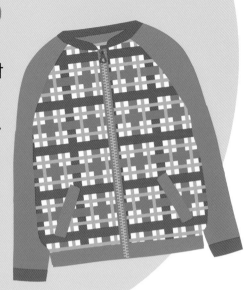

jaguar (noun)

A **jaguar** is a big, wild cat with black spots. It lives in the Americas.

jar (noun)

A **jar** is a small container, usually made of glass. It has a lid and keeps foods such as jelly fresh.

jealous (adjective)

more jealous, most jealous

To feel **jealous** is to feel bad because you want something someone else has.

jeans (noun)

Jeans are trousers made from a tough material called denim. They are often blue.

DICTIONARY DETECTIVE

Which headword contains the word **fish**?

jellyfish (noun)

jellyfish

A **jellyfish** is a sea creature with a soft, round body and long tentacles.

jewel (noun)

A **jewel** is a beautiful, sparkling stone. Some jewels, such as diamonds, cost a lot of money.

jigsaw puzzle (noun)

A **jigsaw puzzle** is a game made from lots of flat pieces that fit together to make a picture.

juice (noun)

Juice is the liquid that comes out of a fruit when you squeeze it.

jump (verb)

jumps, jumping, jumped

When you **jump**, you push both feet off the ground and move suddenly up into the air.

a b c d e f g h i **j** k l m n o p q r s t u v w x y z

Kk

kangaroo (noun)

A **kangaroo** is an Australian animal with big back legs.

Baby kangaroos are called joeys and grow up in their mother's pouch.

key (noun)

A **key** is a specially shaped piece of metal used to lock or unlock a door.

kick (verb)
kicks, kicking, kicked

When you **kick** something, you hit it with your foot.

kid (noun)

1. A child is sometimes called a **kid**.

2. A **kid** is a baby goat.

kind (adjective)
kinder, kindest
Opposites of **kind** are **unkind** and **mean**.

To be **kind** is to say or do something nice for another person.

king (noun)

A **king** is a man who is born to rule a country.

kiss (verb)
kisses, kissing, kissed

To **kiss** someone is to touch them with your lips.

kitten (noun)

A **kitten** is a baby cat.

knife (noun)
knives

A **knife** is a tool used for cutting. Most knives have a handle and a long, sharp metal blade.

koala (noun)

A **koala** is a small, furry animal from Australia. It lives in trees and eats leaves.

DICTIONARY DETECTIVE

Can you find two things on these pages that come from Australia?

a b c d e f g h i j **k** l m n o p q r s t u v w x y z

ladder (noun)

A **ladder** is something you use to climb up high. Ladders are made of metal or wood.

lamb (noun)

A **lamb** is a young sheep that is still with its mother.

large (adjective)

larger, largest
Opposites of **large** are **small** and **tiny**.

If something is **large**, it is big. A hippo is large.

late (adjective)

later, latest
The opposite of **late** is **early**.

To be **late** is to get somewhere after the right time.

lamp (noun)

A **lamp** is a device that gives you light. You can move a lamp around and switch it on and off.

BUS STOP

SCHOOL BUS
STOP

laugh (verb)
laughs, laughing, laughed

To **laugh** is to make noises because you think something is funny.

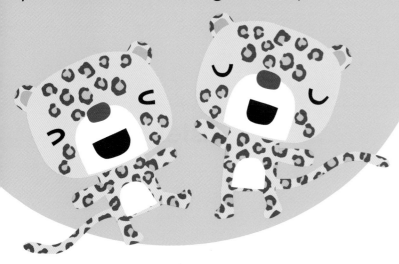

lazy (adjective)
lazier, laziest

The opposites of **lazy** are **hardworking** and **active**.

To be **lazy** is to not want to do work or exercise.

leaf (noun)
leaves

A **leaf** is a flat, green part of a plant, such as a tree.

leg (noun)

Your **legs** are the long parts of your body between your bottom and your feet.

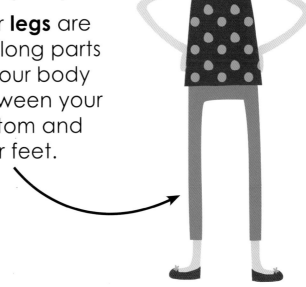

DICTIONARY DETECTIVE

What letter change turns a **lamp** into a **lamb**?

lemon (noun)

A **lemon** is a juicy, yellow fruit with a sour taste.

A
B
C
D
E
F
G
H
I
J
K
L
M
N
O
P
Q
R
S
T
U
V
W
X
Y
Z

letter (noun)

1. A **letter** is a symbol you put with other letters to write words. *A*, *m*, and *z* are all letters.

2. A **letter** is a message someone writes to a friend or relative.

lie (verb)

lies, lying, lay, lain

To **lie** down is to put your body flat on a bed or on the ground.

DICTIONARY DETECTIVE

Can you put these words in alphabetical order?

lizard   lunch   lion

light (adjective)

lighter, lightest

The opposites of **light** are **heavy** and **dark**.

1. If something is **light**, it does not weigh much. It is easy to pick up and carry.

2. If something is **light**, it has pale colors.

lightning (noun)

Lightning is a bright, electric flash that happens during storms.

lion (noun)

A **lion** is a big, wild cat. Lions live in Africa and India.

listen (verb)
listens, listening, listened

To **listen** is to pay attention to a sound or to what someone is telling you.

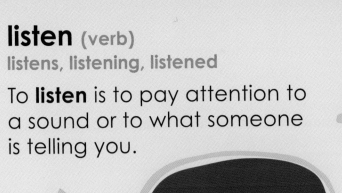

lizard (noun)

A **lizard** is a type of animal with four legs and a long tail.

long (adjective)
longer, longest
The opposite of **long** is **short**.

If something is **long**, its ends are far apart.

loud (adjective)
louder, loudest
The opposite of **loud** is **quiet**.

If something is **loud**, it is noisy and easy to hear.

lunch (noun)
lunches

Lunch is a meal eaten at midday.

a
b
c
d
e
f
g
h
i
j
k
l
m
n
o
p
q
r
s
t
u
v
w
x
y
z

Mm

man (noun)
men

A **man** is a grown-up male person.

map (noun)

A **map** is a drawing that shows you where roads and other places are. You use it to find your way about.

medicine (noun)

Medicine is something you take when you are sick to make you well again.

mermaid (noun)

A **mermaid** is a make-believe creature that looks like a woman with a fish's tail.

midday (noun)

Midday is the middle of the day, or twelve o'clock during the day.

DICTIONARY DETECTIVE

Which headword contains the word **night**?

Which headword contains the word **day**?

midnight (noun)

Midnight is the middle of the night, or twelve o'clock during the night.

milk (noun)

Milk is a white liquid that mother animals make to feed their babies. Many people drink cows' milk.

Monday (noun)

Monday is the first day of the school week. It is the first day after the weekend.

MONDAY	TUESDAY	WEDNESDAY	THURSDAY	FRIDAY	SATURDAY	SUNDAY
	1	2	3	4	5	6
7	8	9	10	11	12	13
14	15	16	17	18	19	20
21	22	23	24	25	26	27
28	29	30	31			

money (noun)

The bills and coins that you use to buy things are types of **money**.

monkey (noun)

A **monkey** is a furry animal that lives in trees. It has a long tail that helps it climb.

a b c d e f g h i j k l **m** n o p q r s t u v w x y z

A B C D E F G H I J K L **M** N O P Q R S T U V W X Y Z

monster (noun)

A **monster** is a scary, make-believe creature.

moon (noun)

The **moon** shines in the sky at night. It is a big ball of rock that moves slowly around Earth about once a month.

moth (noun)

A **moth** is an insect with large wings. It usually flies at night.

DICTIONARY DETECTIVE

Which word is correct?

The **mice** / **mouses** ate your cheese.

mother (noun)

A **mother** is a woman who has children.

motorcycle (noun)

A **motorcycle** is a vehicle with two wheels and an engine.

mountain (noun)

A **mountain** is a very tall, sloped piece of land. It is like a very big hill.

mouse (noun)
mice

A **mouse** is a small, furry animal with a long tail. Mice have sharp front teeth for gnawing food.

mouth (noun)

Your **mouth** is the part of your body you use to talk, eat, and drink.

mushroom (noun)

A **mushroom** is a living thing that looks like a little umbrella. You can eat some mushrooms; others are poisonous.

music (noun)

Music is the sound that people make when they sing or play instruments.

a b c d e f g h i j k l **m** n o p q r s t u v w x y z

A B C D E F G H I J K L M N O P Q R S T U V W X Y Z

narrow (adjective)
narrower, narrowest
The opposite of **narrow** is **wide**.

If something is **narrow**, its sides are close together.

needle (noun)

A **needle** is a long, thin piece of metal used for sewing. It is sharp at one end and has a hole for thread at the other.

nest (noun)

A **nest** is the home that animals such as birds and mice make for their babies.

net (noun)

A **net** is something made from pieces of string or rope tied together with holes in between. Nets are used to catch fish and for games such as tennis and basketball.

new (adjective)
newer, newest
The opposite of **new** is **old**.

If something is **new**, it has just been made. It is not old or worn.

DICTIONARY DETECTIVE

These headwords are spelled wrong. Can you correct them?

numba   noze   nedle

newt (noun)

A **newt** is a small, animal with a long tail. It lives in water and on land.

night (noun)

Night is the time of day between evening and morning. At night, it is dark outside.

nose (noun)

Your **nose** is in the middle of your face. You use it to breathe and smell.

number (noun)

A **number** tells you how many you have of something. Both 3 and 100 are numbers.

nurse (noun)

A **nurse** is a person who takes care of people who are sick or hurt. Nurses often work in hospitals.

Oo

octagon (noun)

An octagon is a shape with eight sides.

octopus (noun)
octopuses or octopi

An **octopus** is a sea creature with eight legs.

oil (noun)

Oil is a greasy liquid that will not mix with water.

OIL

old (adjective)
older, **oldest**
The opposites of **old** are **new** and **young**.

If something is **old**, it was made or born long ago. Old people have been alive for a long time.

old-fashioned (adjective)
more old-fashioned, **most old-fashioned**
The opposite of **old-fashioned** is **modern**.

If something is **old-fashioned**, it looks like it was made long ago.

opposite (noun)

An **opposite** is something that is completely different from something else. The opposite of *over* is *under*.

orange (noun/adjective)
more orange, most orange

1. An **orange** is a round, juicy fruit with orange-colored peel.

2. **Orange** is a color. This carrot is orange.

oven (noun)

An **oven** is the part of an appliance where you roast or bake food.

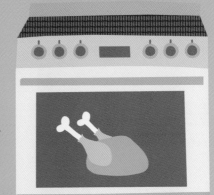

owl (noun)

An **owl** is a bird that hunts for small animals at night. It has big eyes to help it see in the dark.

ostrich (noun)
ostriches

An ostrich is a large bird with a long neck. It cannot fly.

DICTIONARY DETECTIVE

Which words go in the gaps?

An octagon has _____ sides, and an octopus has _____ legs.

a b c d e f g h i j k l m n **O** p q r s t u v w x y z

Pp

paint (noun)

Paint is a colored liquid that you brush onto things to change their color or to make a picture.

pair (noun)

A **pair** of things are two things that go together. We wear a pair of socks.

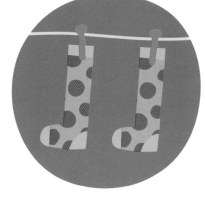

paper (noun)

Paper is a thin, flat material used to write, draw, or paint on. This book is made of paper.

parent (noun)

A **parent** is a mother or a father.

park (noun)

A **park** is a large garden or forest that people can visit.

A
B
C
D
E
F
G
H
I
J
K
L
M
N
O
P
Q
R
S
T
U
V
W
X
Y
Z

parrot (noun)

A **parrot** is a bird with brightly colored feathers and a sharp, curved beak. Some parrots copy the words people speak.

party (noun)
parties

A **party** is an event where people get together to have fun. Some people have birthday parties.

pen (noun)

A **pen** is a long, thin tool that you use to write or draw in ink.

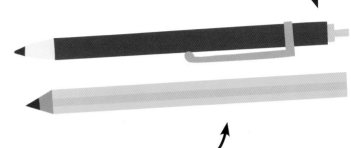

pencil (noun)

A **pencil** is a long, thin stick of wood with black or colored lead in the middle. Pencils are used for writing and drawing.

penguin (noun)

A **penguin** is a seabird with black-and-white feathers. It lives on cold coastlines. It cannot fly but uses its wings as flippers to swim.

DICTIONARY DETECTIVE

Which word rhymes with **carrot**?

a b c d e f g h i j k l m n o **p** q r s t u v w x y z

A B C D E F G H I J K L M N O P Q R S T U V W X Y Z

person (noun)
people

A **person** is a human being. Babies, children, and grown-ups are all people.

pet (noun)

A **pet** is a tame animal that you take care of at home. Dogs, cats, fish, and hamsters are often kept as pets.

DICTIONARY DETECTIVE

Which word goes here?

Many **persons / people** love to play the piano.

photo (noun)

A **photo** is a picture made using a camera. It is short for photograph.

piano (noun)

A **piano** is a musical instrument with black-and-white keys that you push or "touch" to make music.

picture (noun)

A **picture** is a drawing, painting, or photo of something.

pig (noun)

A **pig** is an animal with a fat body, short legs, and a curly tail.

pink (adjective)
pinker, pinkest

Pink is a color. The teapot, wand, and the ballet shoes are pink.

pirate (noun)

A **pirate** is a sailor who attacks and robs other sailors at sea.

plant (noun)

A **plant** is a living thing that grows in soil or in water. Trees, flowers, and grass are all plants.

play (verb)
plays, playing, played

1. When you **play**, you have fun with toys or with friends.

2. When you **play** a sport, you take part in that sport.

3. When you **play** an instrument, you make music with it.

a
b
c
d
e
f
g
h
i
j
k
l
m
n
o
p
q
r
s
t
u
v
w
x
y
z

police officer (noun)

A **police officer** is someone who makes sure people obey the law and who keeps people safe.

present (noun)

A **present** is a gift. It is something special that you give to someone to make them happy.

polite (adjective)
politer, politest
The opposite of **polite** is **rude**.

To be **polite** is to have good manners. If you are polite, you are not rude.

prince (noun)

A **prince** is the son of a king or queen.

princess (noun)
princesses

A **princess** is the daughter of a king or queen.

proud (adjective)
prouder, proudest
The opposite of **proud** is **ashamed**.

To be **proud** is to be pleased with what you or someone else has done.

pumpkin (noun)

A **pumpkin** is a large fruit with orange skin.

puppet (noun)

A **puppet** is a toy figure. You move a puppet by pulling strings or by putting your hand inside it.

puppy (noun)
puppies

A **puppy** is a baby dog.

purple (adjective)
purpler, purplest

Purple is a color. The plums and the cloak are purple.

DICTIONARY DETECTIVE

Which two words on this page have three **p**'s?

Which two words have two **p**'s?

a b c d e f g h i j k l m n o **p** q r s t u v w x y z

A B C D E F G H I J K L M N O P **Q** R S T U V W X Y Z

quarter (noun)

When something is broken into four pieces of the same size, one piece is called a **quarter**.

queen (noun)

A **queen** is a woman who is born to rule a country. A king's wife may also be called a queen.

question (noun)

A **question** is what you ask when you want to know something.

quick (adjective)
quicker, quickest
The opposite of **quick** is **slow**.

To be **quick** is to move or do something fast.

quiet (adjective)
quieter, quietest
The opposites of **quiet** are **loud** and **noisy**.

To be **quiet** is to make very little noise. Someone or something that is quiet is hard to hear.

rabbit (noun)

A **rabbit** is a small, furry animal with long ears and a fluffy tail.

radio (noun)

A **radio** is a machine that picks up and plays music, talk programs, and the news.

rain (noun)

Rain is lots of little drops of water that fall from the clouds.

read (verb)
reads, reading, read

When you **read**, you look at words that are written down and understand them.

rectangle (noun)

A **rectangle** is a shape with four straight sides.

DICTIONARY DETECTIVE

What letter comes after **q** in all the **q** words?

a b c d e f g h i j k l m n o p q r s t u v w x y z

A B C D E F G H I J K L M N O P Q R S T U V W X Y Z

red (adjective)
redder, reddest

Red is a color. The strawberry, rose, and race car are red.

ride (verb)
rides, riding, rode, ridden

To **ride** something like a horse or a bicycle is to sit on it and move along.

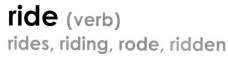

ring (noun)

A **ring** is a round piece of jewelry you wear on a finger.

rhinoceros (noun)
rhinoceroses

A **rhinoceros** is a big animal with tough, leathery skin and one or two horns on its head.

road (noun)

A **road** is a long, hard piece of land that people travel along to reach other places.

robot (noun)

A **robot** is a machine that can do some of the jobs that people do.

rocket (noun)

A **rocket** is the part of a spacecraft that pushes it high into space.

DICTIONARY DETECTIVE

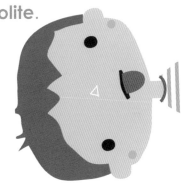

Which headword rhymes with these words?

fun bun sun

rude (adjective)

ruder, rudest

The opposite of **rude** is **polite**.

To be **rude** is to have bad manners.

ruler (noun)

A **ruler** is a long, flat tool used for drawing lines and for measuring how long something is.

run (verb)

runs, running, ran

To **run** is to move along quickly using your legs.

a b c d e f g h i j k l m n o p q **r** s t u v w x y z

Ss

sad (adjective)
sadder, saddest
The opposite of **sad** is **happy**.

To feel **sad** is to feel upset or down.

sandwich (noun)
sandwiches

A **sandwich** is something you eat that is made of two slices of bread with a filling, such as cheese or ham.

DICTIONARY DETECTIVE

Which word is correct?

The green monster is **scarier / scaryer** than the red one.

Saturday (noun)
Saturday is the first day of the weekend. Most children do not go to school on Saturday.

MONDAY	TUESDAY	WEDNESDAY	THURSDAY	FRIDAY	SATURDAY	SUNDAY
	1	2	3	4	5	6
7	8	9	10	11	12	13
14	15	16	17	18	19	20
21	22	23	24	25	26	27
28	29	30	31			

saucepan (noun)

A **saucepan** is a deep, metal cooking pot with a handle and usually a lid.

saw (noun)

A **saw** is a tool with a sharp, jagged edge used for cutting through wood or other hard materials.

scarf (noun)
scarves

A **scarf** is something you wear around your neck to keep it warm.

scary (adjective)
scarier, scariest

If something is **scary**, it is creepy or frightening.

school (noun)

A **school** is a place where children go to learn about things like reading, writing, and numbers.

scissors (noun)

A pair of **scissors** is a tool used to cut paper or cloth. Scissors have two sharp blades and two handles.

see (verb)
sees, seeing, saw, seen

To **see** something is to look at it with your eyes.

SCHOOL

a b c d e f g h i j k l m n o p q r **S** t u v w x y z

A B C D E F G H I J K L M N O P Q R S T U V W X Y Z

shadow (noun)

A **shadow** is a shaded shape on the ground caused by something blocking out the light.

shallow (adjective)

shallower, shallowest
The opposite of **shallow** is **deep**.

If something is **shallow**, its bottom is not far down. A pool or a hole can be shallow.

shark (noun)

A **shark** is a type of big fish. Sharks hunt other sea creatures for food.

sheep (noun)

sheep

A **sheep** is an animal with a thick, woolly coat. Male sheep are called rams, females are called ewes, and babies are called lambs.

shell (noun)

A **shell** is a thin, hard covering around something. Shellfish, snails, eggs, and nuts have shells.

shoe (noun)

Shoes are things you wear on your feet to keep them warm and safe.

shop (noun)

A **shop** is a place where you can buy things, such as food, clothes, or flowers.

FLOWERS

short (adjective)

shorter, shortest
The opposites of **short** are **tall** and **high**.

If something is **short**, its top is close to its bottom.

shorts (noun)

Shorts are short trousers that do not reach your knees.

shout (verb)

shouts, shouting, shouted
The opposite of **shout** is **whisper**.

To **shout** is to yell or speak very loudly.

DICTIONARY DETECTIVE

Can you put these words in alphabetical order?

shark   shorts   shoe

a b c d e f g h i j k l m n o p q r **S** t u v w x y z

shy (adjective)
shyer, shyest

To be **shy** is to be nervous or scared around people you do not know well.

silly (adjective)
sillier, silliest
The opposite of **silly** is **sensible**.

To be **silly** is to act in a funny or not very sensible way.

sing (verb)
sings, singing, sang, sung

To **sing** is to make music with your voice.

skate (verb)
skates, skating, skated

To **skate** is to glide over smooth ground wearing skates, which have blades or wheels on the bottom.

skeleton (noun)

A **skeleton** is all the bones that make up a person's or animal's body.

skip (verb)
skips, skipping, skipped

1. To **skip** is to jump over a rope that is turning around.

2. To **skip** is to hop along, switching from one foot to the other.

skirt (noun)

A **skirt** is a piece of clothing that hangs from your waist and covers all or part of your legs.

DICTIONARY DETECTIVE

Can you use all these words in one sentence?

skeleton   slide   silly

sleep (verb)
sleeps, sleeping, slept

When you **sleep**, you close your eyes and rest deeply. You often dream when you sleep.

slide (noun)

A **slide** is a smooth surface that people move down for fun.

slow (adjective)
slower, slowest

The opposites of **slow** are **fast** and **quick**.

If something is **slow**, it takes a long time to do something. A slow car takes a long time to get places.

a b c d e f g h i j k l m n o p q r **S** t u v w x y z

A B C D E F G H I J K L M N O P Q R S T U V W X Y Z

small (adjective)
smaller, smallest
The opposite of **small** is **big**.

If something is **small**, it is little.

smell (verb)
smells, smelling, smelled

To **smell** something is to find out what it is like by sniffing it with your nose.

smile (noun)

A **smile** is the shape of your mouth when the ends are turned up. You smile when you feel happy.

snail (noun)

A **snail** is a small animal with a shell on its back. It has no legs and moves by sliding on a large foot.

snake (noun)

A **snake** has a long body and no legs. Its skin is scaly.

DICTIONARY DETECTIVE

Which headword rhymes with these words?

tail   pail   mail

snow (noun)

Snow is made of fluffy, white ice crystals that fall from the sky.

snowman (noun)
snowmen

A **snowman** is made of snow and shaped like a person.

sock (noun)

Socks are things you wear on your feet to keep them warm.

soft (adjective)
softer, softest
The opposites of **soft** are **hard** and **firm**.

If something is **soft**, it is easy to shape or bend. Blankets are soft.

space (noun)

Space is the rest of the universe beyond Earth. There is no air in space.

a b c d e f g h i j k l m n o p q r **S** t u v w x y z

spider (noun)

A **spider** is a small animal with eight legs. Most spiders spin webs to catch insects for food.

spoon (noun)

A **spoon** is a tool used for eating. It has a long handle and a round end. You use a spoon to eat foods such as soup and cereal.

square (noun)

A **square** is a shape with four straight sides that are all the same length.

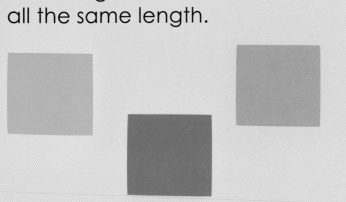

squirrel (noun)

A **squirrel** is a small, furry animal that lives in trees. It has a bushy tail and eats nuts.

star (noun)

1. A **star** looks like a small, bright light in the night sky. It is really a huge, faraway ball of burning gas.

2. A **star** is a shape with five or more points.

steal (verb)
steals, stealing, stole, stolen

To **steal** something is to take something that does not belong to you.

stomach (noun)

Your **stomach** is the part of your body where food goes after you chew it. It helps break up food.

strawberry (noun)
strawberries

A **strawberry** is a soft, sweet red fruit with seeds on it.

strong (adjective)
stronger, strongest
The opposite of **strong** is **weak**.

If something is **strong**, it is powerful or hard to break. A strong person can carry heavy loads.

sun (noun)

The **sun** is a close star that shines in the sky and gives Earth light and heat. Earth moves around it.

DICTIONARY DETECTIVE

Which headword is made up of these letters? **g t o n s r**

a b c d e f g h i j k l m n o p q r **S** t u v w x y z

Sunday (noun)

Sunday is the second day of the weekend. Many people do not work or go to school on Sunday.

supermarket (noun)

A **supermarket** is a large shop that sells many different kinds of food.

swan (noun)

A **swan** is a large bird with a long neck. It lives on rivers and lakes.

swim (verb)
swims, swimming, swam, swum

To **swim** is to move through water. People swim using their arms and legs.

swing (verb)
swings, swinging, swung

When something **swings**, it is hanging down and moving back and forth.

W
X
Y

Tt

table (noun)

A **table** is a piece of furniture with legs and a flat top.
You can eat or work at a table.

tadpole (noun)

A **tadpole** is a young frog or toad. It hatches with gills and a tail but with no legs.

tail (noun)

An animal's **tail** grows at the end of its body. It helps the animal balance.

talk (verb)
talks, talking, talked

To **talk** is to speak, or to use words, out loud.

tall (adjective)
taller, tallest
The opposite of **tall** is **short**.

If something is **tall**, its top is high above the ground.

DICTIONARY DETECTIVE

Which headword contains the word **super**?

a b c d e f g h i j k l m n o p q r s t u v w x y z

A B C D E F G H I J K L M N O P Q R S **T** U V W X Y Z

taste (verb)
tastes, tasting, tasted

To **taste** something is to find out what it is like by putting it in your mouth.

teacher (noun)

A **teacher** is a person who helps other people learn things.

telephone (noun)

A **telephone** is a machine you use to talk to someone in another place.

television (noun)

A **television** is a machine that shows pictures on a screen and also has sounds.

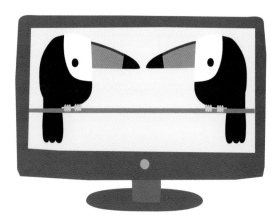

tell (verb)
tells, telling, told

To **tell** someone something is to talk to them about it.

tent (noun)

A **tent** is a shelter made of a piece of cloth stretched over poles. You use a tent for camping.

thermometer (noun)

A **thermometer** is something you use to find out how hot or cold a person, place, or other thing is.

DICTIONARY DETECTIVE

Which two headwords start with the letters **tele**?

thin (adjective)

thinner, thinnest
The opposite of **thin** is **fat**.

To be **thin** is to be skinny, or to weigh very little.

third (noun)

When something is broken into three pieces the same size, one piece is called a **third**.

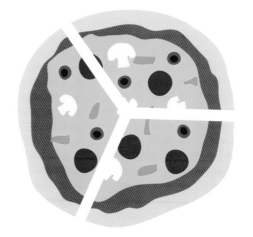

thunder (noun)

Thunder is a loud sound in the air that you hear after lightning.

a b c d e f g h i j k l m n o p q r s **t** u v w x y z

A B C D E F G H I J K L M N O P Q R **S** **T** U V W X Y Z

Thursday (noun)

Thursday is the fourth day of the school week.

MONDAY	TUESDAY	WEDNESDAY	THURSDAY	FRIDAY	SATURDAY	SUNDAY
	1	2	3	4	5	6
7	8	9	10	11	12	13
14	15	16	17	18	19	20
21	22	23	24	25	26	27
28	29	30	31			

tiger (noun)

A **tiger** is a big, wild cat with orange-and-black striped fur. Wild tigers are rare, but some still live in India and China.

tiny (adjective)

tinier, tiniest

The opposites of **tiny** are **huge** and **big**.

If something is **tiny**, it is very small.

tired (adjective)

more tired, most tired

To be **tired** is to need a rest or to feel sleepy.

toe (noun)

Your **toes** are part of your foot. Each foot has a big toe and four smaller toes.

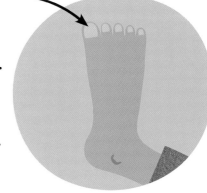

DICTIONARY DETECTIVE

Which word is correct?

Don't touch **tomatoes / tomatos** with your toes.

tomato (noun)
tomatoes

A **tomato** is a soft, round red fruit that people often eat in salads.

tool (noun)

A **tool** is something you use to make work easier. Wrenches, screwdrivers, and hammers are all tools.

toothbrush (noun)
toothbrushes

You use a **toothbrush** with toothpaste to keep your teeth clean.

top (noun)

A **top** is something you wear on the upper half of your body. A T-shirt is a top.

touch (verb)
touches, touching, touched

To **touch** something is to find out how it feels using your fingers.

a
b
c
d
e
f
g
h
i
j
k
l
m
n
o
p
q
r
s
t
u
v
w
x
y
z

A B C D E F G H I J K L M N O P Q R S **T** U V W X Y Z

towel (noun)

A **towel** is a piece of soft, thick cloth that you use to dry yourself.

tractor (noun)

A **tractor** is a farm vehicle with big back wheels. It is often used to pull things.

toy (noun)

A **toy** is something you play with. Dolls, kites, teddy bears, and train sets are all toys.

train (noun)

A **train** is a line of cars with an engine that moves along tracks.

trampoline (noun)

A **trampoline** is a piece of play equipment with a stretchy surface. You use it to jump high into the air.

tree (noun)

A **tree** is a tall plant with leaves, branches, and a thick wooden stem, called a trunk.

truck (noun)

A **truck** is a large, strong vehicle that takes things from one place to another.

BIG TRUCK CO.

triangle (noun)

A **triangle** is a shape with three straight sides.

Tuesday (noun)

Tuesday is the second day of the school week.

MONDAY	TUESDAY	WEDNESDAY	THURSDAY	FRIDAY	SATURDAY	SUNDAY
	1	2	3	4	5	6
7	8	9	10	11	12	13
14	15	16	17	18	19	20
21	22	23	24	25	26	27
28	29	30	31			

trousers (noun)

Trousers are things you wear. They cover part of your body and each leg.

DICTIONARY DETECTIVE

Can you put these words in alphabetical order?

train   truck   tractor

a b c d e f g h i j k l m n o p q r s **t** u v w x y z

A B C D E F G H I J K L M N O P Q R S T U V W X Y Z

uniform (noun)

A **uniform** is a set of clothes that show what job, school, or sports team you belong to.

umbrella (noun)

You hold an **umbrella** over your head to keep yourself dry when it rains.

underwear (noun)

We call the clothes that we wear under all our other clothes **underwear**. Briefs are underwear.

unicorn (noun)

A **unicorn** is a make-believe animal that looks like a horse with a horn on its head.

upside down (adjective)

If something is **upside down**, its top is closer to the ground than its bottom.

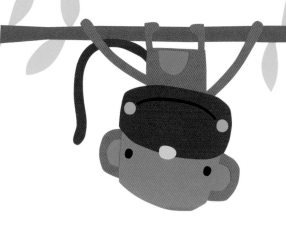

vacuum cleaner (noun)

A **vacuum cleaner** is a machine that sucks up dust and dirt.

vase (noun)

A **vase** is a container that you can use to hold cut flowers in water.

vegetable (noun)

A **vegetable** is part of a plant that can be eaten. We cook vegetables and also eat some raw. Cabbages, carrots, and onions are vegetables.

violin (noun)

A **violin** is a musical instrument made of wood. You play it using a bow.

volcano (noun)
volcanoes

A **volcano** is a mountain that sometimes erupts, sending out gases and melted, or molten, rocks.

DICTIONARY DETECTIVE

Can you use all these words in one sentence?

unicorn   volcano   upside down

a b c d e f g h i j k l m n o p q r s t u **V** w x y z

wake (verb)
wakes, waking, woke, woken

To **wake** up is to stop being asleep. We wake up each morning.

walk (verb)
walks, walking, walked

To **walk** is to move along by putting one foot forward and then the other.

wash (verb)
washes, washing, washed

To **wash** something is to make it clean. We wash our hands with soap and water. We wash clothes in a washing machine.

watch (noun)
watches

A **watch** is a small clock that you can wear on your wrist. It tells you what time it is.

watch (verb)
watches, watching, watched

To **watch** something is to look at something.

water (noun)

Water is a clear liquid found in rivers, lakes, and oceans. It also comes out of faucets.

wave (verb)
waves, waving, waved

To **wave** is to move your hand from side to side to mean hello or goodbye.

weak (adjective)
weaker, weakest
The opposite of **weak** is **strong**.

If something is **weak**, it breaks easily or it has little power or strength.

Wednesday (noun)

Wednesday is the third day of the school week. It is the middle day of the workweek.

MONDAY	TUESDAY	WEDNESDAY	THURSDAY	FRIDAY	SATURDAY	SUNDAY
	1	2	3	4	5	6
7	8	9	10	11	12	13
14	15	16	17	18	19	20
21	22	23	24	25	26	27
28	29	30	31			

wet (adjective)
wetter, wettest
The opposite of **wet** is **dry**.

If something is **wet**, it has water on or in it.

DICTIONARY DETECTIVE

Which headword rhymes with these words?

make lake take

a b c d e f g h i j k l m n o p q r s t u v **W** x y z

wheel (noun)

Wheels are round and can turn. Bicycles, cars, and trains all have wheels so that they can move.

whisper (verb)

whispers, whispering, whispered
The opposite of **whisper** is **shout**.

To **whisper** is to talk very quietly.

white (adjective)

whiter, whitest

White is a color. The mouse is white.

wide (adjective)

wider, widest
The opposite of **wide** is **narrow**.

If something is **wide**, its sides are far apart.

wind (noun)

Wind is air that is moving. You cannot see it, but you can see the things it moves.

wing (noun)

A **wing** is a part of an insect, bird, or plane that helps it fly.

woman (noun)
women

A **woman** is a grown-up female person.

wolf (noun)
wolves

A **wolf** is a wild animal that looks a bit like a large dog.

worry (verb)
worries, worrying, worried

To **worry** is to think about bad things that might happen.

write (verb)
writes, writing, wrote, written

To **write** is to use a pencil or a pen to record words or numbers.

DICTIONARY DETECTIVE

Which word is correct?

A pack of **wolves / wolfs** lives in the forest.

a b c d e f g h i j k l m n o p q r s t u v **W** x y z

X-ray (noun)

An **X-ray** is a picture that lets a doctor or dentist see inside your body.

xylophone (noun)

A **xylophone** is a musical instrument with a row of bars of different lengths.

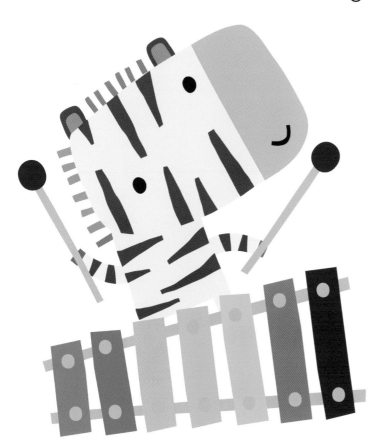

yacht (noun)

A **yacht** is a boat with sails or an engine. Yachts are used for fun.

yawn (verb)
yawns, yawning, yawned

When you **yawn**, you open your mouth wide and breathe out.

yellow (adjective)
yellower, yellowest

Yellow is a color. The banana, cheese, and duckling are yellow.

yogurt (noun)

Yogurt is a food made from milk. It is often mixed with fruit.

yolk (noun)

The **yolk** is the middle part of an egg. It is yellow.

young (adjective)
younger, youngest
The opposite of **young** is **old**.

To be **young** is to have lived for only a short time. Children are young.

yo-yo (noun)

A **yo-yo** is a round toy that you roll up and down on a string.

DICTIONARY DETECTIVE

Which word goes here?

I am **young**, but a baby is _____ than me.

a b c d e f g h i j k l m n o p q r s t u v w x y z

zebra (noun)

A **zebra** is an animal that looks like a horse with black-and-white stripes. Zebras live in Africa.

zipper (noun)

A **zipper** joins two pieces of material together. The zipper's teeth lock together when you close it.

zoo (noun)

A **zoo** is a place where people can go to see wild animals.